LITTLE CRITTER®
STORYBOOK COLLECTION

🔹 A Big Tuna Trading Company, LLC/J. R. Sansevere Book
www.harperchildrens.com   www.littlecritter.com

LITTLE CRITTER®

STORYBOOK COLLECTION

BY MERCER MAYER

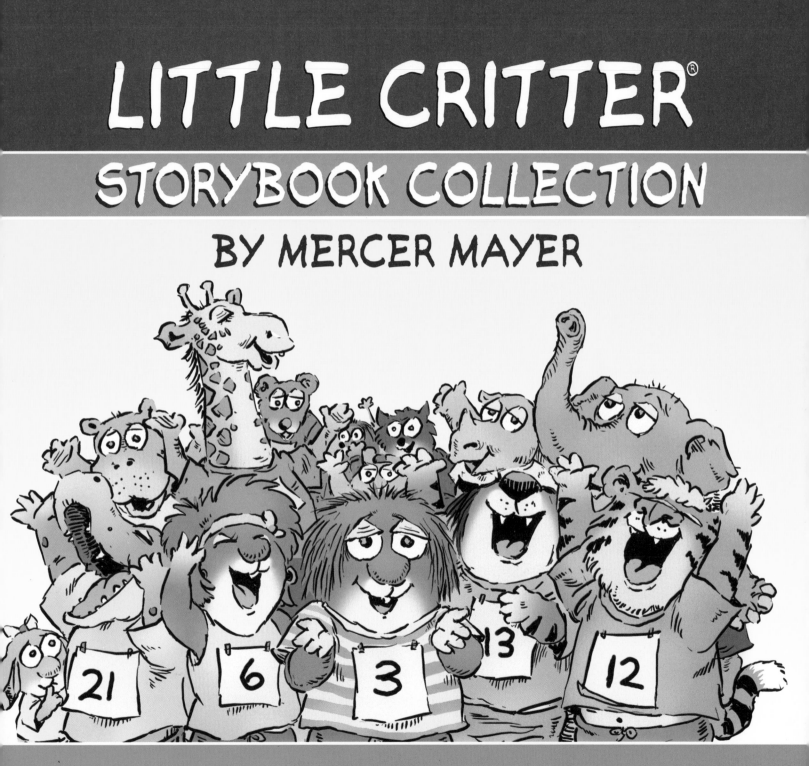

HarperFestival®
A Division of HarperCollinsPublishers

Table of Contents

A Letter from Little Critter:

Hi! I'm Little Critter, and this book is all about me!

I live in Critterville with my family. I have lots of pets. I have a dog and a cat and a mouse and a grasshopper and a spider and a frog. And a snake and a bunch of fish and some turtles, too.

I go to Critterville Elementary School. I am in first grade. Miss Kitty is my teacher; she is really nice. Going to school is fun because I get to see my best friends Tiger and Gator.

I do lots of things after school, like play baseball

and football and ride my bike and my skateboard. In the summertime, I go fishing with my grandpa and go to the beach with my grandma.

This book has lots of stories: I spend the weekend with Grandma and Grandpa, make a project for the school science fair, get ready for a big race and learn about eating healthy, enjoy a snowy day, build a growing machine, become the captain of a tugboat, and drive a dump truck. Let's start reading!

I hope you enjoy my book!

BYE-BYE, MOM AND DAD
BY MERCER MAYER

Today Mom and Dad went on a trip, and Grandma and Grandpa came to stay with us.

"Bye-bye, Mom and Dad!" I said. "Don't worry. I will take care of everything."

First, we had to do our chores. So, we vacuumed . . .

. . . we mopped

. . . and we dusted.

Then we did some painting. I told
Grandpa I was a very good painter,
but the paint spilled a little.

Then we had to do some shopping. At the store,
I pushed the cart . . .

. . . and showed Grandma just what we needed to buy.

When we got home, I made a special lunch for everyone—peanut butter and pickle sandwiches . . .

. . . with potato chips, marshmallows, and chocolate syrup on top.

Grandma and Grandpa said it was the best lunch they ever had.

After lunch, Little Sister helped Grandpa water the garden while Grandma and I did the dishes.

"You have to use lots of soap if you want to get the dishes really clean, Grandma," I said.

Then we went to the movies. Grandma likes popcorn and Grandpa likes candy . . .

. . . so we had to get lots of both.

23

After that, we went bowling. I helped Grandma roll
the ball because it was too heavy.

On the way home we were hungry, so we stopped at Critter Burger.

I ordered a Super Burger and a Super Shake, but I dropped them.

When we got home, it was time to get ready for bed.
So we all put on our pajamas . . .

. . . washed our faces

. . . and brushed our teeth.

"Mom says to use lots of toothpaste," I said.

Then I told Grandma and Grandpa a scary story.
It was a little too scary for them, so we had to check
for monsters in the closet and under the bed.

Grandma and Grandpa were still a little scared, so
Little Sister and I stayed with them all night long.
Good night, Grandma! Good night, Grandpa!

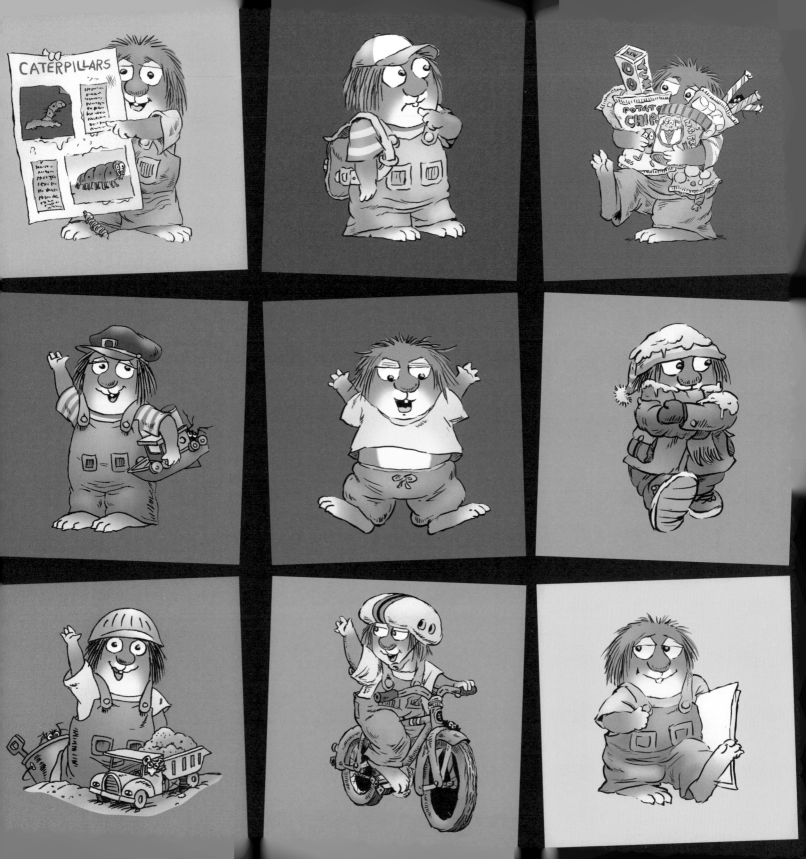

GOOD FOR ME AND YOU
BY MERCER MAYER

*To Caleb and
Justine McNair
with love*

Today in school we learned about what foods are good for us.

I asked why carrots are better for me than cookies.

"Because carrots have vitamins to help you grow," Miss Kitty told me. "Cookies just taste good."

In gym, we did lots of exercises. First, we jumped rope. I jumped the fastest, but the rope was a little too long.

We had a contest to see who could do the most sit-ups and push-ups. I won—almost.

The next day, I made lunch for Mom, Dad, and Little Sister. "Surprise!" I said. "Eat every bite, because all of this food is good for you."

After lunch, I told my family I had another surprise. I took them all on a bike ride.

"Come on, Dad!" I said. "You can do it!"

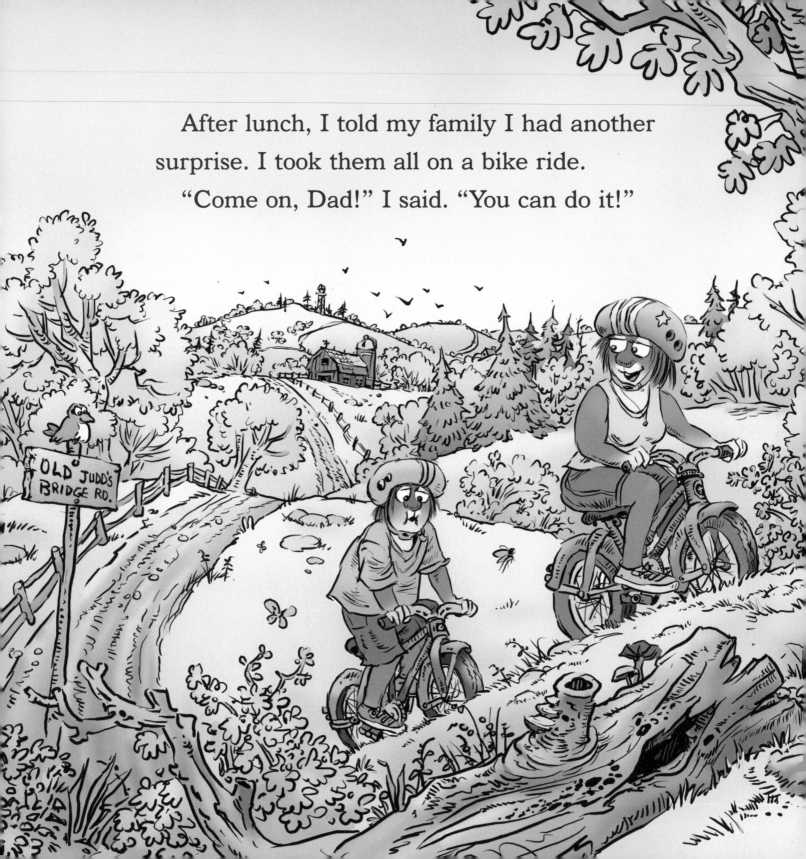

The next day when Tiger came over to play
video games, I had a great idea.

44

I called all of our friends
to tell them.

Me and my friends played football all afternoon. I scored the touchdown that won the game.

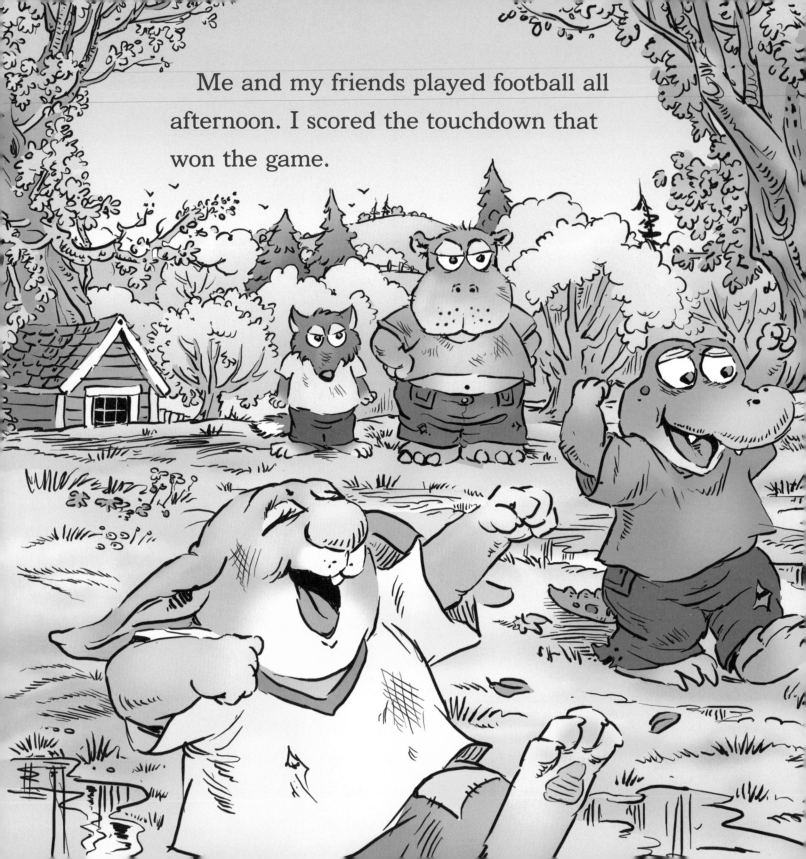

The next morning, I walked to school
instead of taking the bus. I had to hurry
because walking sure takes longer.

At lunch, I almost had a brownie for dessert,
but I decided to have an apple instead.

On the way home, we saw a big sign.

"Look," said Gabby. "There's going to be a race in Critterville."

"Let's run in the race!" I said.

Everybody cheered.

Gabby said we should do
exercises to get ready for the race.
But then I got hungry, so I
stopped to have a snack.

Tiger and Malcolm were hungry, too, so I gave each
of them a snack. Exercise sure gives you a big appetite.

The next day, we went swimming. I wore my snorkel and my flippers because they make me go faster.

After that, we practiced running as fast as we could.
I beat Tiger . . .

. . . but Gator beat me.

Malcolm beat all three of us . . .

. . . but Gabby beat Malcolm. Gabby's really fast.

The day of the race, we all took our places at the starting line.

"On your marks, get set, go!" called the announcer.

Then he blew a whistle.

I got off to a fast start.

I didn't win, but I ran the whole way without stopping. Doing stuff that's good for you isn't just healthy, it's lots of fun, too.

JUST A TUGBOAT
BY MERCER MAYER

We like to play with boats.
When I get bigger, I am going to
be a tugboat captain. . . .

Smoke puffs out of the tugboat's smokestack. *Puff! Puff!* Then I sail my tugboat out of the harbor all the way . . .

. . . to the ocean. I see a big ship that needs help getting to the harbor. I blow my whistle. *Toot! Toot!*

Everyone onboard the ship waves
at me. Then I tug and pull and
push that big ship all the way . . .

. . . into the harbor.
Smoke blows out of the tugboat's smokestack. *Puff! Puff!* Everyone cheers as they get off the big boat.

Next I pull a big tanker out of the
harbor. I blow my whistle. *Toot! Toot!*
I pull the tanker all the way . . .

. . . to the ocean.
Then I wave as the big
tanker sails away.

Puff, puff goes my smokestack.
Toot, toot goes my whistle, as I sail my tugboat back to the harbor to pull the next big ship on its way.

It is fun to play with boats.

Splash! Splash! Toot! Toot! Puff! Puff!

JUST A SCHOOL PROJECT
BY MERCER MAYER

We were having a science fair at our school. Miss Kitty said we're each supposed to do a special project.

Tiger was going to
do his about rocks.

Gator was going to
do his about stars.

Gabby was going to
do hers about horses.

Everyone had an
idea except for me.

I told Mom I needed an idea for my project, so she took me to the library.

The librarian showed me the science section.
There were lots and lots of books, and they gave me
lots and lots of ideas.

THIS IS LAUNCH

KEEP CLEAR

OFFICIAL ROCKET SHIP

First, I made a rocket ship. But no matter how hard I tried, I didn't fly to the moon.

Then, I decided to dig for dinosaur bones. I dug and dug, but all I found was one of my dog's chewing bones.

After that, it was time for lunch. And there, right
next to my sandwich, was a caterpillar.

"Mom! Dad!" I shouted. "I know what I'm going to do my project about—caterpillars!"

Dad helped me look up facts about caterpillars.

Did you know that a caterpillar starts its life as an egg? When it hatches, it eats leaves and flowers all day and all night long.

So, I went outside and hunted for caterpillars.

They sure were hard to find.

I put the caterpillars in a special box with some leaves and some flowers so they would have enough to eat.

Dad and I went to the store to get poster board, markers, and glue. You sure need lots of stuff when you do a project.

I wrote my report on the poster board, but I wrote a little too big. Dad had to go back to the store and get more poster board.

Then I drew some pictures of caterpillars and glued them onto my report, but the glue was a little too sticky.

Did you know that a caterpillar gets bigger by splitting its skin down the back and crawling out in a new skin?

A week later, it was time for the science fair.
Everyone brought in a project.

I set up my poster board . . .

. . . and opened up the box with the caterpillars in it.
And you know what?

A whole bunch of butterflies flew
out! That's because caterpillars turn
into butterflies when they grow up!
It was the best science project ever!

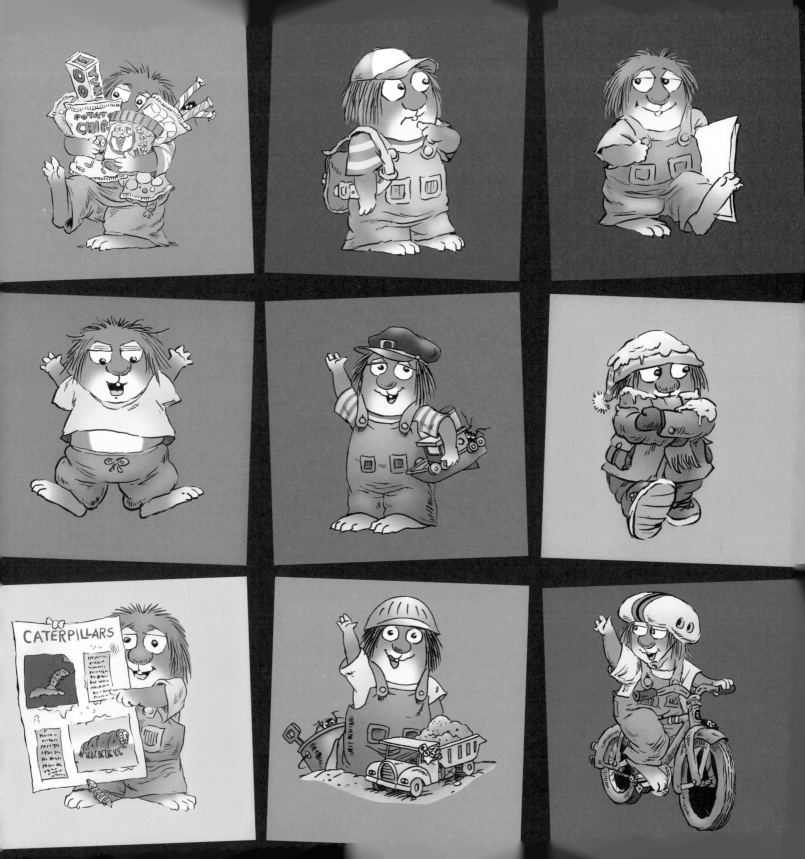

JUST A DUMP TRUCK

BY MERCER MAYER

We like to play with trucks.

When I get bigger, I'm going to drive
a dump truck . . .

I climb up the side of my truck to get
into the cab.

Then I turn on the engine.
Vroom! Vroom!

I beep my horn and wave to everyone!

Beep! Beep! I drive to a construction site.

The digger fills up my dump
truck with rocks and dirt. I
drive the dirt and rocks away . . .

. . . and dump them out.

Whoosh! Whoosh! The bulldozer

rolls over the dirt and rocks.

I drive to another place, where
the digger fills my bed with little
rocks called gravel.

I dump the gravel at a different construction site where a new building is being built.

All day long I drive my dump truck back and forth, carrying loads . . .

. . . and dumping them.
Whoosh! Whoosh!

It's fun to play with trucks. *Beep! Beep!*
Vroom! Vroom! Whoosh! Whoosh!

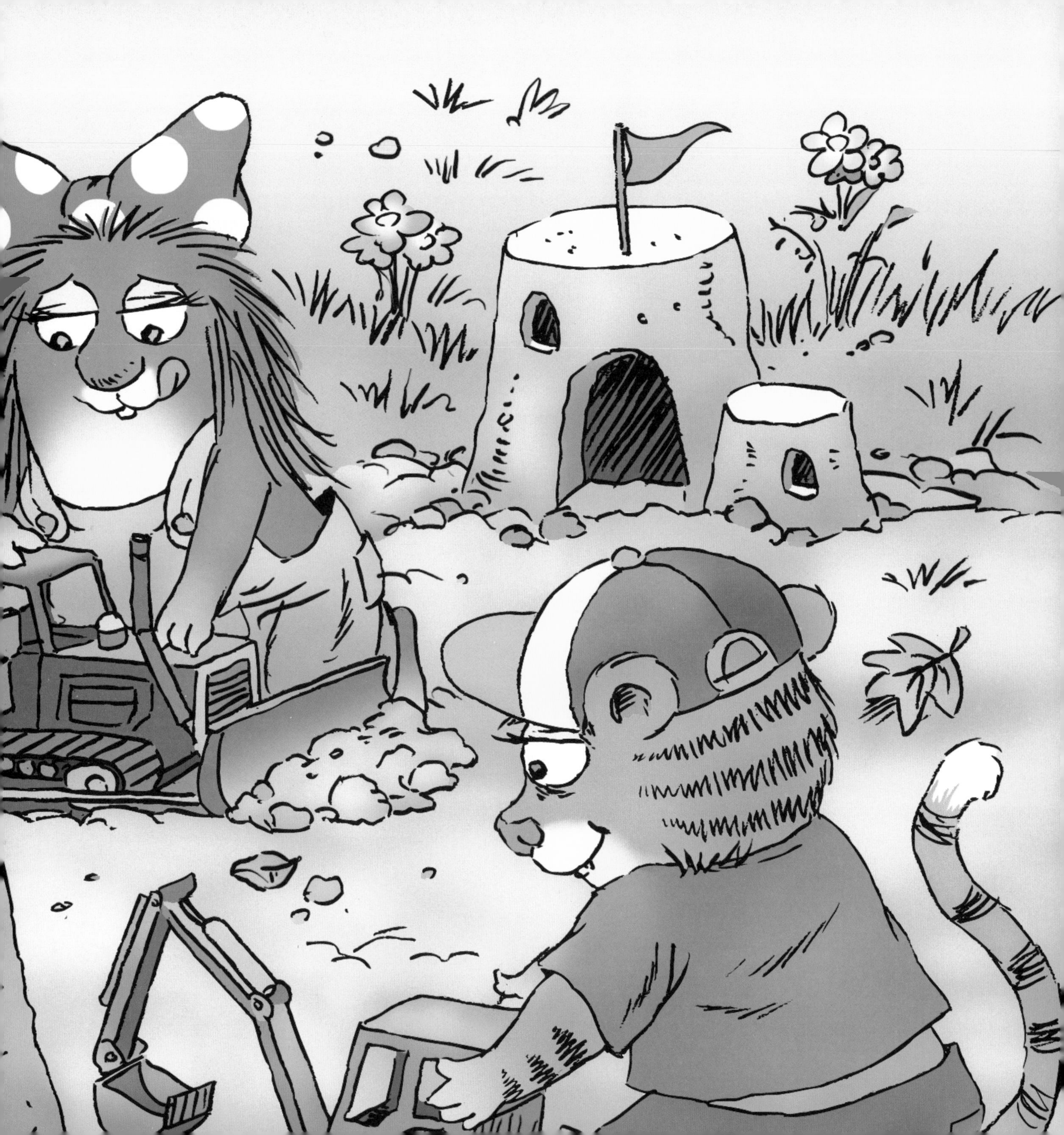

JUST A SNOWMAN
BY MERCER MAYER

To Trent Birkins

It snowed and snowed all night long, so today we had a snow day. Hooray!

I wanted to build a snowman. I put on my snow
boots and my hat and my mittens and my scarf.

Then, I helped Little Sister
put on her snow stuff.

After that, Dad needed
my help. We shoveled and
shoveled lots of snow . . .

. . . and then we had to find the car.

I was going to build a snowman next, but Little Sister wanted to have a snowball fight. I let her hit me a bunch of times.

I only hit her one time by accident.

So then, I had to say I was sorry
and give her a big hug.

I was going to build a snowman after that, but Tiger and Bun Bun wanted to go ice-skating.

So, I showed everyone how I can skate backwards . . .

. . . and do jumps.

Then Tiger and I raced.
It was a tie.

I was ready to build a snowman next, but
Maurice and Molly wanted to go sledding.
I steered all the way down the big hill. Watch
out, Maurice and Molly, here we come!

When Little Sister and I got home, I was going to build a snowman. But Gator wanted me to help him build a snow fort.

And then Gabby wanted to make snow angels.

Finally! It was time to build a snowman. First, we made a big snowball for the bottom.

Next, we put a smaller one on top . . .

. . . and an even smaller one on top of that one.

Little Sister added prunes for his eyes
and mouth, and a carrot for his nose.

And I put Mom's scarf around his neck and Dad's hat on his head. I even let him wear my sunglasses. Our snowman sure looked great!

Little Sister was getting cold so we went inside. The
snowman looked cold, too, so I decided to make some
of my special hot chocolate to warm us all up.

142

First, Mom heated some milk while I got out the secret ingredients.

I put everything into the pot and
stirred it all up with a big spoon.

Then I put marshmallows on top and I poured the hot chocolate into three big mugs—one for me, one for Little Sister . . .

. . . and one for the snowman. It was the best snow day ever. I sure hope it snows again tomorrow!

JUST BIG ENOUGH

BY MERCER MAYER

Every morning on my way to school, I always sit in the same seat on the school bus. But this morning . . .

. . . a big kid took my seat.

"Excuse me," I said. "You're sitting in my seat."
The big kid didn't move. I guess he didn't hear me.

At recess, I wanted to play football with the big kids,
but they said I couldn't play because I was too small.

And at lunch, the big kids took all of the cupcakes. They laughed when I said they had to share. They told me the cupcakes were just for them.

"I wish I were bigger," I said to my friends.
They nodded.
"I bet there are lots of ways to grow," I said.

After school, my mom measured me.

"How can I make myself grow?" I asked Mom.

"Eat your vegetables," she said. "They will make you big and strong."

So at dinner, I ate almost all my spinach and a whole
bunch of carrots.

"Am I bigger yet?" I asked Mom.

"Not yet," said Mom.

Later, I asked Dad what would make me grow.
"Exercise," he said.

So, I did jumping
jacks . . .

sit-ups . . .

. . . and push-ups
. . . and I ran around and
around.

After all that exercise
I didn't get any bigger,
but I sure got tired.

That night, I couldn't sleep. So, I read a comic book.
And that's when I got a great idea.

The next morning, I asked Dad for some wood and some glue. Mom gave me tinfoil. And Little Sister let me have a jar of her glitter.

"What are you making?" asked Little Sister.

"A growing machine," I said.

I worked on the growing machine all morning. When
it was finished, I sprinkled glitter on it so it
sparkled like the one in the comic book
I had read.

I made a helmet out of tinfoil.

Then I put on my helmet and climbed into the growing machine.

I sat in the growing machine
all afternoon.

I even ate my
lunch there.

When it became dark, Dad said it was time to come home.

"Did I grow?" I asked.

Dad shook his head and said, "Not yet."

"Maybe I should sleep in the growing machine," I said.
Dad didn't think that was such a good idea.

The next day, I went to Grandma and Grandpa's farm.

"What's the matter, Little Critter?" asked Grandpa.

I told Grandpa about the big kids and how I was trying
to get big, too, so that I could do all the things the big
kids did.

Grandpa took me out to the meadow.
"Look at those two horses," he said.
"Which one do you think is the fastest?"
"The big one!" I said.

Grandpa let the big horse and the little horse loose.
They started to run across the field.

And do you know which one was the fastest?
The little one.

The next day at school, the big kids said again that I couldn't play football because I was too small. I started to get mad.

"I challenge you to a relay race," I said. "The big kids against the little kids."

The big kids laughed, but they said okay.

The whole school came to watch the race.

And you know what?

The little kids won!

So, I guess sometimes being small is
just big enough.